THE ROYAL KINGDOM

By

SUNDAS SHAKEEL

(Clinical Psychologist)

2024

THE ROYAL KINGDOM

First edition. November 2, 2024.

ISBN: 979-8227014016

Written by Sundas Shakeel.

CHAPTERS

DEDICATION

This book is dedicated to all those reader who have faced trauma and have found the strength to overcome their obstacles. As a psychologist, my aim to motivate and inspire others through these pages, encouraging them to learn from their past and grow stronger after each challenge. Life's difficulties often feel overwhelming, but they also offer the opportunity for renewal and growth. Every setback is not the end; it is a stepping stone to something new. I hope this book provides comfort and motivation for those who need to hear that they can rise again, no matter how many times they fall. Every ending brings the chance for a fresh start, and the journey toward healing is one of resilience, hope, and renewal. You are capable of turning your pain into power and moving forward with courage.

ACKNOWLEDGEMENTS

First and foremost, I am deeply thankful to Almighty Allah for countless blessings and for giving me the strength, wisdom, and inspiration to complete this book. Without Allah's guidance, this achievement would not have been possible, and I am forever grateful for mercy and grace. Writing this book has been a journey that I could not have completed alone. First and foremost, I would like to thank my Parents for their unwavering support and encouragement throughout this process.

A special thank you to my mentors and colleagues, whose insights and feedback have shaped my understanding and enriched the content of this work. Your guidance has been invaluable. I am also deeply grateful to my friends for their patience and understanding, especially during the times when my focus on this project may have pulled me away from other commitments. Lastly, to my readers, thank you for taking the time to engage with my work. It is my hope that the stories and insights shared here will inspire and motivate you on your own journey.

Sundas Shakeel

INTRODUCTION

Prince Ronaldo was born into a royal family, the only cherished child of his beloved parents. Gifted with exceptional powers from birth, he quickly became the pride of his family and a symbol of hope for the kingdom. His father, King Eric, was admired for his fair and just rule, and under his leadership, the kingdom flourished. The people respected him, and his wisdom was celebrated far and wide. However, this fame and respect created a rift within the royal bloodline. King Eric's first cousin, Michael, grew resentful of his cousin's success and admiration. For Michael, Eric's popularity was unbearable, a constant reminder of the power and influence he lacked. This envy soon turned into a deep-seated desire to seize the throne. Driven by greed, Michael launched a surprise attack on the kingdom. In one swift strike, he claimed the throne, forcing King Eric's family to flee and leaving young Ronaldo without a home or a kingdom to call his own. Prince Ronaldo's life took a drastic turn as he went from royalty to a humble villager, learning resilience and strength while planning his return to reclaim his rightful kingdom. As Ronaldo grew, he was determined to reclaim his rightful inheritance. His journey was fraught with challenges, but he never wavered in his resolve. Throughout this quest, he found strength not only in his courage but also in the unwavering loyalty of his supporters, who believed in him and his right to the throne. Their loyalty became a cornerstone of his journey, fueling his determination to confront Michael and restore justice. The loyalty and faith of his companions were indispensable, reminding Ronaldo that he was not alone in this struggle. Their support became the greatest motivation for him as he faced obstacles that seemed insurmountable. Without this loyalty, his journey to reclaim the kingdom would have been impossible. Ultimately, it was through courage, loyalty, and persistence that Prince Ronaldo found the strength to pursue his goal and honor his father's legacy.

Key words

Royal family, Exceptional powers, King Eric, Just rule, Flourishing kingdom, Resentmen, Greed and envy, hrone seizu, Forced exile, Humble villager, Resilience and strength, Rightful inheritance, Quest for kingdom, Loyalty of supporters, Courage and persistence, Confronting Michael, Restoring justice, Honoring legacy

Chapter # 1

Peaceful Environment of the Kingdom

Once upon a time, there was a kind and humble king and queen who ruled a prosperous kingdom. They were loved by their people for their fairness and compassion. Despite their wealth and power, their greatest treasure was their only son, Prince Ronaldo. From a young age, Ronaldo displayed extraordinary qualities that set him apart from other children.

He had some magical abilities, such as the power to control and manipulate animals simply by looking into their eyes and freeze humans. He could also sense when someone was hiding something, no matter how well they tried to conceal it. These abilities made him special, but they also made him vulnerable. The king Eric and queen Madonna, knowing that their son's powers could make him a target, kept them a secret from everyone in the kingdom. They wanted to protect Ronaldo and ensure that no harm would come to him because of his unique gifts.

Only a few trusted individuals were aware of his magical talents, one of them being his devoted nanny, Liya had been with the royal family since before Ronaldo was born. She was a loyal and wise woman, tasked with supervising the palace staff. Though she had two sons of her own, she loved Prince Ronaldo dearly, treating him as if he were her own child. Her youngest son was the same age as the prince, and the two boys often played together, forming a bond of friendship that mirrored the love and care Liya felt for the prince.

Liya was one of the few people the king and queen trusted completely with the secret of Ronaldo's powers. Her loyalty to the royal family was unwavering, and she ensured that no one in the palace discovered the truth about the prince. She watched over him with a careful eye, protecting him from any threat that might arise. Her love for the prince and her understanding of the dangers his powers could bring made her an essential part of his life.

As Ronaldo grew older, his powers became stronger, and the need for secrecy grew even more crucial. The king, queen, and Liya worked together to protect the prince, ensuring that his magical abilities remained hidden from the world, keeping him safe from those who might seek to harm him.

In the Royal Kingdom, a place filled with happiness, justice, and peace, the people lived harmoniously under the rule of a kind and just king and queen. They believed in serving humanity and ensuring the welfare of every individual in their kingdom. Among their children was a young boy named Ronaldo, who was just seven years old. He was a gentle soul, full of curiosity and love for the world around him.

Ronaldo had a close companion, his loyal nanny, Liya, who was always by his side, protecting him and teaching him about the ways of life. Ronaldo loved Liya deeply, seeing her as more than a caregiver; he loved her like a mother. Ronaldo had a special bond with animals, especially his favorite pet, a small creature that he cared for dearly. He spent much of his time in the vast royal gardens, exploring the wonders of nature and playing with his pet. The gardens were lush with greenery, full of flowers, and teeming with life. Birds chirped in the trees, butterflies fluttered by, and the soft rustling of leaves in the wind made it a magical place for a child like Ronaldo.

One bright and sunny day, while playing in the garden, Ronaldo noticed a small sparrow flying from one place to another. Its delicate wings flapped rapidly as it darted between the branches of a tree. Ronaldo watched the bird with wide eyes, fascinated by its movements. He stood still, observing as the sparrow flew closer and then quickly darted away when he moved toward it.

Curious about the bird's behavior, Ronaldo turned to Liya, who was sitting nearby, always watching over him. "Liya, why does the sparrow fly away when I come close to it?" he asked, his innocent voice full of wonder. "Where does it live?" Liya smiled gently at the young prince's question. She adored Ronaldo's inquisitive nature and his deep affection for animals. With a soft voice, she explained, "Dear Prince, the sparrow flies away when humans come near because it knows that humans can sometimes be harmful to it. It's protecting itself from danger."

Ronaldo tilted his head, trying to understand what Liya was saying. "But why would humans want to harm the sparrow?" he asked, puzzled. In his young mind, he could not fathom why anyone would want to hurt such a small, beautiful creature. Liya nodded thoughtfully before responding. "Not all humans are the same, my dear Ronaldo. Some people are kind and love animals, just like you. But others may not be as gentle and might harm creatures without realizing the damage they are doing." She paused, seeing the concerning Ronaldo's face.

"The sparrow builds its nest in trees because houses are made for humans

to live in. The trees and skies are where the birds find their home, a place they feel safe." Ronaldo thought about this for a moment, looking up at the sparrow now perched high in the tree. He loved animals and couldn't imagine hurting them. His young heart ached at the thought of someone harming the sparrow.

"Liya, I don't want to harm the sparrow," Ronaldo said softly, his eyes reflecting the compassion in his heart. "I want to protect it. I love birds and animals. Will I be able to keep them safe when I grow older?"

Liya smiled warmly, her heart swelling with pride at the boy's kind words. "Of course, my dear Ronaldo," she replied. "I know you will grow up to be a brave and wise prince, and you will protect all the animals and birds of the kingdom. They will be safe because of your love for them." Roanldo smiled back at Liya, feeling a sense of purpose. "Yes, Liya. I will make sure all the birds are safe when I grow older. I'll be like you, caring for everyone."

Liya's eyes softened, and she gently patted Rolanldo's head. "I know you will, my prince. The world will be a better place because of your kindness." As they sat together in the garden. Ronaldo's heart filled with determination. He continued to watch the sparrow, vowing silently to protect all creatures, big and small. In that moment, the young prince's future seemed brighter than ever, a future where his love for nature would guide him to become a compassionate and just ruler, just like his parents.

Chapter # 2

King Eric and Queen Madonna's Papularity and Michael's Jealousy

In the heart of the Royal Kingdom, King Eric was celebrated far and wide for his sense of justice. Unlike many rulers, he didn't treat people according to their social standing or wealth but judged them based on their deeds and character. His fairness made him beloved by the common folk and respected by the noblemen. It was said that under his reign, even the poorest citizen could seek justice in his court and receive it without bias.

The King's reputation spread across neighboring lands, earning him the title of "The Just King." However, not everyone was pleased with King Eric's popularity. His cousin, Michael, harbored a deep resentment toward him. Michael had always been envious of Eric's success and the respect he garnered from their subjects. While the kingdom praised Eric for his wisdom and fairness, Michael stewed in bitterness. He despised the way everyone looked up to the king and wished for that admiration to be his.

Michael's jealousy only grew with time, and he secretly began to plot against his cousin. His envy turned into an obsession, and he spent years devising a plan to dethrone Eric and take the kingdom for himself. Each time Michael visited the palace, his eyes scanned the surroundings with hatred. He looked upon the bustling court, the thriving city, and the loyal subjects who revered the king, all with a heart full of malice.

In every encounter with Eric, Michael would speak in a harsh and bitter tone, veiling his resentment only slightly. His words were often sharp, criticizing the king's decisions or mocking his ideals of fairness. To those who didn't know him well, Michael's behavior might have seemed rude or impulsive. But to those who knew him closely, it was clear that his actions stemmed from a deep well of jealousy and frustration.

Despite Michael's venomous words and attitude, King Eric paid little heed to his cousin's behavior. The king was a patient man, more concerned with the well-being of his people than the petty jealousy of his kin. Whenever Michael spoke out of turn or behaved disrespectfully, Eric would either change the subject or dismiss his cousin's remarks as mere outbursts of frustration.

To Eric, Michael's words were like the bark of a harmless dog; annoying but not Worth his attention. Unbeknownst to King Eric, Michael's plotting was far from harmless. While the king remained focused on governing his kingdom with justice and compassion, Michael was busy forming alliances with those who were dissatisfied with Aric's reign. He whispered in the ears of noblemen who had grievances with the king, convincing them that they would fare better under his rule.

Slowly but surely, Michael's plan began to take shape. For years, Michael bided his time, careful not to raise too much suspicion. He was confident that one day, he would succeed in his scheme. He believed that by overthrowing King Eric, he would finally achieve the power and recognition he had always craved. What he didn't realize, however, was that his jealousy was blinding him to the very qualities that made Eric a great ruler.

While Michael focused on seizing power, Eric's strength lay in the love and loyalty of his people something that could not be stolen. Michael had always been an ambitious man, his mind constantly scheming for power. The Royal Kingdom, with its vast wealth and influence, had long been a coveted prize. However, his rise to power had not come through bravery or sheer strength but rather through careful manipulation

and deception. His planning, though cheap and seemingly reckless, was soon to turn into reality.

The foundation of Michael's plan was the betrayal of those closest to the king. For months, Michael had carefully infiltrated the inner circle of the court. Among the king's most trusted advisors, there were a few whose loyalty wavered under the promise of wealth and influence. Michael had sensed this weakness and exploited it to his advantage. His allies within the palace secretly relayed critical information to him, from guard shifts to the layout of the king's chambers, ensuring that his attack would be swift and unexpected.

As Michael's helper in this devious plan, my role was to ensure the pieces of his strategy aligned perfectly. I had spent weeks working in the shadows, cultivating relationships with key individuals in the kingdom guards, servants, and even low ranking nobles. These people unknowingly provided me with small but essential details: the best times to strike, which gates were left unguarded during the late hours, and where the most vulnerable points of the palace security lay.

The night of the attack, I coordinated the movements of Michael's men. While the king and queen were asleep in the safety of their royal chambers, I ensured that the guards stationed nearby were either bribed or distracted. I also planted misinformation, leading the palace guards to believe that an enemy force was gathering at the far outskirts of the kingdom.

This successfully diverted many of the kingdom's forces, leaving the palace exposed. Under the cover of darkness, Michael led his small but deadly force into the palace. Thanks to the treachery of the king's trusted men, the gates were opened without resistance. By the time the king and queen awoke to the chaos, it was too late. Michael's plan had been executed flawlessly, and the kingdom was his for the taking.

The cheapness of his planning no longer mattered. The Royal Kingdom had fallen, not by strength, but by cunning betrayal. Michael's sudden attack was shocking and completely unacceptable. It happened without warning, catching everyone off guard. The king Eric, queen Madonna, and prince were all in their respective rooms, unaware of the brewing danger. None of them had the slightest idea of what was about to unfold. The attack was swift, leaving little time for anyone to react. Michael's actions shattered the peace that had surrounded the royal family. The atmosphere, once calm and secure, became one of chaos and fear.

As the news of the attack spread through the palace, panic took over. No one could comprehend what had driven Michael to such a terrible act. The royal family, having been caught off guard, now faced the daunting task of confronting the aftermath.

The shock of the incident lingered in the air, leaving everyone questioning what might come next. Michael reached the king room, he swiftly took down to the all guards stationed outside.

Listening to the noises, King stepped outside He saw his injured guards lying on the floor and realized the severity of the situation. As chaos reigned around him, the king desperately tried to protect himself, knowing that his safety was now precarious. The once secure palace had become a perilous battleground. Michael attack king with his sward, and murder him on the spot. Then Michael entered queen was alone, he killed the queen, and left the room.

Chapter # 3

Michael's Attack on Kingdom and Prince Ronaldo's New Journey

Michael's next target was Prince Ronaldo. Driven by ambition and a thirst for power, he moved swiftly toward the prince's chambers, determined to end Ronaldo's life and claim victory. However, Liya, a woman of compassion and courage, had already sensed the impending danger. Out of kindness and loyalty to the prince, she swiftly took action.

Liya, with the help of her elder son, devised a plan to get Ronaldo to safety. They worked quickly and silently, knowing time was of the essence. Together, they managed to smuggle Prince Ronaldo out of the palace, away from Michael's clutches. Liya's heart raced as they guided him through secret passages, ensuring that no one would suspect their escape. Her elder son, strong and resourceful, played a crucial role, navigating the hidden routes to evade detection.

They eventually sent the prince to a remote village, far from the reach of Michael's forces. It was a quiet, unassuming place, where Ronaldo could blend in and stay hidden. Liya knew that this was the only way to save his life. When Michael reached Ronaldo's room, his rage was palpable.

Finding it empty, he realized the prince had slipped through his fingers. Enraged, he ordered his soldiers to search every corner of the kingdom. "Find him immediately!" he commanded, his voice filled with fury. His men scoured the palace and the lands beyond, but to no avail. Prince Rolando had vanished. Despite Michael's aggressive orders and the relentless hunt, Liya's quick thinking and bravery had succeeded. Prince. Ronaldo was safe, at least for now, hidden away in the quiet village, far from the dangers of the palace.

After the tragic attack on King Eric and his family, Michael took control of the kingdom. He announced that, sadly, no one from the royal family had survived the assault. As King Eric's first cousin and closest living relative, Michael claimed his right to the throne. With the kingdom in a state of shock and mourning, he swiftly assumed leadership, promising stability and protection in these uncertain times.

Though questions lingered about the circumstances of the attack, Michael's ascension was seen by many as a necessary step to ensure the kingdom's future and maintain in order. Michael's careful and thrifty planning had led to his success, though it came at a cost to those around him. Prince Ronaldo, raised in a quiet village as a common boy, remained hidden from the political machinations that threatened his life. His humble upbringing had kept him safe, but it also left him unaware of the power and danger that loomed over him.

Liya, on the other hand, had proven herself a loyal servant throughout this ordeal. She had always been true to her duties, ensuring the safety and well being of the prince, even if it meant putting herself in danger. Her devotion to the cause was unwavering, and she would have given her life to protect.

Ronaldo. However, this dedication came with unintended consequences. Michael, despite his success, had grown suspicious of everyone around him. His paranoia led him to question even his most trusted allies, and Liya became a target of his doubt. He began to suspect that she had hidden the prince, possibly to undermine his plans or to protect Ronaldo from his growing ambitions.

This suspicion was enough for Michael to act. In a swift and calculated move, he had Liya arrested, accusing her of treason and conspiracy. Her loyalty, once admired, was now seen as a threat. The woman who had done everything to ensure the prince's safety now found herself imprisoned, her fate uncertain. Despite this, Liya's resolve remained strong. Even in chains, she knew she had done the right thing in protecting the true heir. But now, it was up to fate to decide her next steps, as Michael's grip tightened and the prince's future hung in the balance.

Ronaldo was a child who had been given a second chance at life. Orphaned at a young age, he found a new home with a humble couple from a small village. This couple, despite their deep love for each other, had never been blessed with children of their own. Their lives had been marked by the quiet yearning for the pitter patter of little feet, the laughter of a child, and the warmth that a family brings.

When Ronaldo entered their lives, it was as if a long held dream had finally come true. The couple, simple villagers with hearts full of love, saw in him the embodiment of their hopes and desires. Though Ronaldo was not their flesh and blood, they embraced him as their own. In their eyes, he was not just an adopted child; he was their miracle, their answered prayer.

They loved Ronaldo with a depth and sincerity that knew no bounds. Every day, they showered him with affection, providing him with not only the basic necessities of life but also an abundance of warmth and care. They taught him the values of kindness, hard work, and respect, ensuring that he grew up not just in comfort, but with a strong moral foundation.

To the couple, Ronaldo was a prince. Not in the literal sense, but in the way they treated him. Their devotion to him was so profound that they spared no effort in ensuring his happiness and well being. The villagers often remarked on the couple's transformation after adopting Ronaldo.

They had always been kind hearted, but now, with Ronaldo in their lives, they seemed to radiate a newfound joy and purpose. For Ronaldo, the love and attention he received from his adoptive parents was something he cherished deeply. Though he had come from difficult beginnings, he found solace and belonging in their care. He knew that while they might not share the same blood, they shared something far more precious: a bond of love and family.

In the quiet village, this small family of three became an example of the power of love and the beauty of adoption. Ronaldo, for the couple, was not just a son but the realization of a dream they had long thought impossible. And in him, they found the fulfillment of their greatest wish.

Chapter # 4

Ronaldo's Interaction with Stranger and manipulating the horse

King Michael's reign was not well received by the public. Known for his rigid stance, he imposed harsh policies that burdened the common people, earning their discontent. His rule was characterized by a lack of compassion, and few in the kingdom spoke favorably of him.

The kingdom seemed to languish under his leadership, with his stern rule alienating the very people he was meant to serve. Meanwhile, Prince Ronaldo, the king's son, was growing older. Years had passed, and now Ronaldo had blossomed into a young adult. Though he lacked formal education, his heart was pure, and he embodied many of the virtues associated with children.

Humility was one of his defining traits, a reflection of the values his adoptive parents had instilled in him from an early age. Despite his lack of schooling, Ronaldo possessed a unique gift an exceptional power that set him apart from others. This mysterious ability was something that both Ronaldo and his parents were aware of, though it had yet to fully manifest in a way that could benefit the kingdom. The power lay dormant, waiting for the right moment to reveal its true potential. Unlike King Michael, Ronaldo was well liked by those who knew him. His natural humility and kindness won the hearts of many.

Though he lacked the knowledge of governance and royal matters, his intrinsic goodness hinted at a brighter future for the kingdom. In time, many began to hope that Ronaldo's ascent to the throne would bring about much needed change, lifting the oppressive policies of King Michael and restoring peace and prosperity to the land.

One day, Ronaldo found himself alone in the forest, enjoying the tranquility of his surroundings. As he wandered deeper, he noticed a stranger sitting atop a tall, powerful horse. The stranger, without any hesitation, boldly entered the land that belonged to Ronaldo's family. Intrigued but cautious, Ronaldo approached the man, who greeted him with a harsh and condescending tone.

The stranger was arrogant, his words filled with disdain as he refused to acknowledge his mistake of trespassing on private property. He dismissed Ronaldo's attempts at a civil conversation and instead chose to threaten him, as though he had some authority over the situation. His eyes were cold, and his demeanor intimidating, but Ronaldo remained calm and observant.

As the tension mounted, the stranger stepped forward, assuming Ronaldo would back down. However, Ronaldo did something unexpected. His gaze shifted to the horse, and in a moment of silent command, he manipulated the animal with just his eyes. The horse, as if understanding Ronaldo's silent request, began to move restlessly, unsettling the stranger.

Before the man could react, the horse turned abruptly and bolted out of the land, taking its rider with it. The stranger, now in shock and disbelief, clung to the reins, desperately trying to regain control. Fear crept into his mind as he glanced back at Ronaldo, realizing this was no ordinary man.

There was something mysterious and powerful about him, something beyond comprehension. Afraid and unnerved, the stranger hurried away, never looking back, fully aware that he had encountered someone far beyond his expectations. A stranger returned to the city after an unusual encounter in a remote village. The incident was strange and intriguing enough that he immediately shared it with his friends. Among his friends was a well known TV anchor named Anna, renowned for hosting a popular show that invited people with extraordinary or unique qualities those who stood out from the common crowd.

As the stranger recounted his experience, the Anna listened intently. He spoke of a villager who had left a strong impression on him, describing the unusual events and the villager's unique traits. The anna's curiosity piqued as she realized this story was unlike anything she had featured before. Excited about the potential of boosting her show's ratings, she quickly formulated a plan. This villager was not just a person of interest but someone whose story could captivate a wide audience. It was a rare and fascinating case, something her viewers would find both surprising and entertaining.

The idea of showcasing a simple villager with such a compelling backstory seemed perfect for the kind of content her show thrived on stories that broke away from the ordinary. As a media professional always seeking fresh angles, she decided to invite the villager to appear on her program. She envisioned the episode drawing immense publicity, knowing that such a case was bound to make waves and generate buzz. Filled with excitement, the anchor couldn't wait to reach out to the villager and bring his story into the limelight, turning an ordinary man into a momentary celebrity.

This rare opportunity was something she was eager to capitalize on, promising great success for her show. The anna received a critical mission: she had to locate and retrieve a specific person. Without hesitation, she prepared herself for the task at hand, knowing time was of the essence. The urgency of the situation drove her to act swiftly, leaving little room for error. After receiving the person's address, she meticulously planned her journey, ensuring everything was in place before she set off.

For days, she worked diligently, gathering resources and information, studying the route to her destination, and mentally preparing herself for any obstacles she might face along the way. With determination, she set out, her focus unwavering. Each step brought her closer to the location, as she carefully navigated through unknown terrains and unfamiliar cities.

Finally, after days of travel, she reached her destination. The address she had obtained was correct, and now, the most critical part of her mission lay ahead: confronting the person and bringing them back safely. She stood outside the door, her mind sharp, heart steady, and ready to execute the next phase of her mission.The journey had been long, but the real challenge was just beginning. Now, it was time to face whatever awaited her beyond that door. With a deep breath, she knocked, ready to complete her mission and fulfill the duty she had been entrusted with.

Chapter # 5

Ronaldo's Attraction towards Anna

After several days of effort, Anna finally found the Ronaldo she had been searching for. When he met her, he was immediately captivated by her charm and poise. Ronaldo a simple villager with a modest lifestyle, had never encountered someone like her before. Her urban sophistication and confidence left a lasting impression on him. He was struck by her beauty and intelligence, falling in love with her at first sight. Despite his humble background, Ronaldo's sincerity and authenticity caught the anchor's attention.

In their conversations, she discovered a unique depth in him his stories of rural life, his wisdom shaped by nature, and his pure outlook on the world. The contrast between their lives fascinated her. Though she lived in the fast paced world of media, she found something refreshing in Ronaldo's simplicity.

Over a few more meetings, the anna began to see more than just a story in him. She realized that his life experiences, though vastly different from hers, were valuable and worth sharing with the world. She admired his honesty and strength, qualities that stood out amidst the noise of modern life. Gradually, she convinced Ronaldo to step out of his comfort zone and appear on her show for an interview.

Although hesitant at first, Ronaldo agreed, encouraged by her warmth and encouragement. The idea of being interviewed felt daunting to him, but his growing feelings for the anchor gave him the courage to take the leap. What began as a chance encounter evolved into a meaningful connection, with the promise of something more, both professionally and personally.

Anna had always shown a soft spot for Roanldo, making him believe that she liked him. In truth, however, her intentions were far from genuine. Anna had a plan she needed to take Roanldo with her to the city, and her affection was merely a means to an end. Ronaldo, unaware of her real motives, fell for her act. He approached his parents, asking for permission to leave with Anna, promising to return in a few days. His parents were reluctant, knowing something Rolando himself had forgotten.

Years ago, when Ronaldo was just a child, a tragedy occurred that wiped his memory of his real life and family. His current parents, though not his biological ones, had raised him with love and care. They knew the truth but had kept it hidden for Ronaldo's sake, fearing that the reality of his past would shatter him.

His biological family, long gone, was a memory lost to him, but his adoptive parents had always felt a deep sense of duty to protect him. When Ronaldo asked for permission to leave, they hesitated. They didn't want him to go, knowing that the city could uncover truths that had been buried for years. They tried to dissuade him, but Ronaldo was firm, enchanted by Anna's attention and the promise of adventure.

Despite their unease, they reluctantly agreed, but deep down, they feared what this journey might reveal about his forgotten past. They knew he would not simply return unchanged after a few days, and the path ahead was full of uncertainties. Ronaldo's parents had been deeply worried about him. They feared that if anyone discovered his true identity, he might be harmed. Their concerns grew stronger as time went on, but Ronaldo remained unaware of just how right they were.

One day, Ronaldo overheard a conversation between a news anna and her assistant that changed everything. The anna confessed to her assistant that she had used Ronaldo, pretending to care about him only to get an exclusive interview. She had created false narrative, feigning love and affection, just to manipulate him. Ronaldo was shocked and deeply hurt by this revelation. Feeling betrayed, Ronaldo confronted the anchor, his emotions boiling over. "I can't believe you would do this to me," he said, his voice filled with pain. "You pretended to care, just for an interview. You used me. After this, I don't think I'll ever be able to trust a girl again."

His words were heavy, filled with disappointment and disillusionment. "You've hurt me more than you can imagine. All for your career. Well, go back to your fake world. My village isn't a place for someone like you." With that, Ronaldo turned away, walking back to his simple, quiet life, his heart bruised but wiser. "Thank you for this lesson," he added, a bittersweet acknowledgment of the painful experience.

He realized that not everyone who came into his life had genuine intentions, and this hard lesson would stay with him. He would no longer be so easily fooled. His village, and his heart, would be guarded from now on. Anna sat alone, her thoughts swirling in a storm of regret. The confrontation with Ronaldo had been a disaster, and now she found herself grappling with the weight of her actions. She had acted impulsively, letting her emotions get the best of her, and now the consequences were

painfully clear. Ronaldo had been more than patient, but her behavior crossed a line that even his understanding could not overlook.

Each memory of their interaction replayed in her mind, and she cringed at her own words and actions. She had been harsh, her criticism unfair and unwarranted. The realization of how deeply she had hurt him gnawed at her conscience. Anna had always respected Ronaldo's perspective, and to see him so distant now, his trust shattered, was a bitter pill to swallow. She knew that an apology was in order, but every attempt to bridge the gap seemed futile.

Ronaldo had made it clear that he could not accept her apologies, and each rejection stung more than the last. The door to reconciliation felt firmly shut, and she was left in the painful knowledge that her actions had irrevocably altered their relationship.

Anna's heart ached as she understood the full extent of her mistakes. She wanted to make amends, to show how deeply she regretted her actions, but it seemed that the chance for forgiveness had slipped through her fingers. All she could do now was live with the consequences of her behavior and hope that, in time, the wounds she had inflicted might heal, even if Ronaldo could never forgive her.

Chapter # 6

Reveals Hidden Reaity

Liya's elder son, after many years of separation, finally went to meet his mother, who had been imprisoned by Michael for a long time. The reunion was filled with emotion, but Liya's mind was focused on a more urgent matter. As soon as they embraced, she inquired about Ronaldo, her other child who had been raised by an adopted family. With a stern and resolute tone, Liya instructed her son to find Ronaldo and deliver an important message to his adoptive parents. She told him, "This is the right time to reveal the truth to Ronaldo about his past. He deserves to know everything."

Liya believed that now, as an adult, Ronaldo was ready to face the reality of his origins and the injustices that had been done to their family. She went on to explain that Ronaldo was the rightful heir to everything that had been taken from them by Michael. She emphasized that Ronaldo had to claim what was rightfully his because he was the true owner of their family's legacy.

Liya had been waiting for this moment, and now that Ronaldo was mature enough, she felt it was time for him to fight for what belonged to him. Her son listened carefully, understanding the weight of the task. He knew that delivering this message would not only change Ronaldo's 's life but also ignite a confrontation with Michael, the man who had torn their family apart. As he left his mother, he promised to carry out her wishes and prepare Ronaldo for the difficult truths that lay ahead.

After Liya's son Darius moved to meet Ronaldo, he finally reached his destination with a heart full of determination. He carried Liya's message, and with it, the weight of truth that had long been hidden. Ronaldo's adopted parents had been waiting for this moment, but they were not fully prepared for the emotional consequences. The time had come to tell Ronaldo the truth about his past, a truth they had guarded for so long, fearing it would change everything.

As Darius spoke, the air grew heavy with tension. The adopted parents listened quietly, their hearts heavy with sorrow. They had always known this day would come, but the reality of it was harsher than they had imagined. They feared what would follow once the truth was revealed. Would Ronaldo still see them as his parents? Would the bond they had nurtured all these years break?

Despite their pain, they knew they couldn't keep the truth hidden any longer. Ronaldo deserved to know who he truly was. They had raised him with all the love and care they could offer, but deep inside, they had always known that one day he might leave them to seek his real family.

The thought of being alone again, after all the years they had spent together, was deeply painful. They had already been alone once, before they adopted him, and now the fear of returning to that loneliness gnawed at them. But they also understood that this was not about them. It was about Ronaldo's future and his right to know where he came from. As much as it hurt, they had to let him go. The reality was harsh, but they believed that in time, he would find peace with the truth.

They could only hope that, no matter where his journey led him, he would remember the love they had shared and not leave them behind entirely. Ronaldo's world shattered the moment he heard the truth. He had always believed his life was built on a strong foundation his parents, the ones who had raised him with love and care. But now, the revelation left him numb and disoriented.

The people he had called his parents all his life, the ones who nurtured him and filled his childhood with warmth, were not his biological parents. The truth was difficult to comprehend. It felt as if his entire identity was a lie. Everything he thought he knew about himself was suddenly in question. As he processed the news, a whirlwind of emotions engulfed him. He was shocked, hurt, and confused. How could the people he trusted most keep such a life altering secret from him?

At the same time, he felt a deep sense of sadness for his real parents those who he had been separated from without knowing. What had happened to them? Why had his life turned out this way? These questions gnawed at him, and the pain of not knowing was almost unbearable.

However, what dominated his emotions the most was anger. His mind fixated on Michael, the man who had been at the center of so many of his life's problems. Michael had always been a thorn in Ronaldo's side, an arrogant to figure who made life harder for him at every turn.

Now, with the revelation of his true origins, Ronaldo was convinced that Michael was somehow responsible for all of his misery. The thought of Michael and the control he seemed to exert over Ronaldo's life filled him with rage determined not to remain a victim, Ronaldo resolved to take control of his life. He would no longer allow Michael to dictate his fate. He was no longer the confused boy who followed without question. Now that he knew the truth, Ronaldo felt empowered. He was determined to claim his rightful place, to confront Michael, and to ensure that the arrogant man could no longer manipulate or dominate him.

This was Ronaldo's moment of transformation. His life, which had just been turned upside down, now had a new purpose. He would never let anyone control his destiny again. Ronaldo made the decision to confront the person responsible for his parents' death. Determined and filled with emotion, he knew this encounter would change everything. The pain and anger he'd carried for years now drove him forward, seeking both answers and closure from the one who caused his suffering.

Ronaldo made the decision to confront the person who murder and responsible for his parents' death. Determined and filled with emotion, he knew this encounter would change everything. The pain and anger he'd carried for years now drove him forward, seeking both answers and closure from the one who caused his suffering.

Chapter # 7

Ronaldo's Preparation for Battle, against Michael

Ronaldo was preparing himself for the upcoming battle with Michael, driven by a deep inner pain that stemmed from the loss of his family. This sorrow, a constant ache in his heart, served as both a reminder of his suffering and a source of unwavering motivation. Every waking moment was consumed with thoughts of vengeance and redemption. The memory of his loved ones fueled his determination, pushing him to become stronger with each passing day. In the months leading up to the inevitable clash, Ronaldo dedicated himself entirely to mastering the art of combat.

He sought out the finest teachers and spent countless hours training with swords, honing his skills until they became second nature. The blade felt like an extension of his body, and his movements became fluid and precise. But swords were not his only focus; he also trained in the use of other weapons, each tool becoming another means to achieve victory in the upcoming battle.

Ronaldo's training went beyond physical preparation. He conditioned his mind to remain sharp and focused, knowing that his emotions could not cloud his judgment when the time came. He had to be strategic, calculating every move to ensure he would come out victorious. The thought of facing Michael, the one responsible for his family's demise, kept him pushing harder, testing the limits of his endurance.

Though his heart ached with sorrow, Ronaldo found strength in that pain. It was the fire that kept him moving forward, the force behind every swing of his sword. As the day of the battle drew closer, he knew that all his pain and sacrifice would culminate in one final confrontation. Victory wasn't just for him it was for his family, and nothing would stop him from achieving it. As time passed, his curiosity grew stronger. After many days of struggling, he finally gathered the courage to confront Michael, ready to face whatever came his way. Determined and resolute, he knew the moment had come to put his doubts behind him and meet Michael head on.

Ronaldo's parents were filled with a mixture of pride and sorrow as they prepared to send their son off on a journey that would shape his future. They had watched him grow, nurtured his dreams, and now they stood by, hoping that the world would be as kind to him as they had been. Their hearts swelled with hope, wishing that he would find success in the mission he was about to undertake. It was a journey filled with challenges and uncertainty, yet they had full faith in his ability to conquer whatever came his way.

As they bid him farewell, their eyes brimmed with tears. It wasn't just a physical goodbye; it was an emotional parting, one filled with hopes, dreams, and prayers for his success. His parents knew that the road ahead would not be easy, but they had instilled in Ronaldo the values of hard work, resilience, and determination. These qualities, they believed, would guide him through even the toughest of trials. Their love and belief in him were unshakable, and though it pained them to see him leave, they knew that this was a necessary step toward his growth.

Their silent prayers accompanied him as he set off. They whispered wishes for his safety, strength, and unwavering focus. They believed deeply that one day, he would return triumphant, having achieved his goals and fulfilled the dreams they had for him. Ronaldo, too, carried their love in his heart. He had promised them that once he achieved his target, once he had secured the success he sought, he would return and take his parents along with him, ensuring that they could enjoy the fruits of his labor together.

With each step he took toward his mission, he knew that he was not walking alone. His parents' hopes, their faith, and their love were with him every moment, driving him forward. Ronaldo's goal was not just about personal achievement; it was about honoring the sacrifices his parents had made for him. In his heart, he had already decided that his victory would be their victory too, and when the time came, they would all share in the joy of his success, together forever.

Upon reaching the gates of his long forgotten kingdom, Ronaldo felt a surge of emotions overwhelm him. The sight of the towering castle and the familiar landscape stirred memories he had buried deep within himself. As he stood there, a wave of nostalgia washed over him, taking him back to his childhood.

The faces of his loved ones appeared, though blurred and distant, like the fading remnants of a dream. He could almost hear the laughter of his younger self echoing through the corridors, the innocence of youth untouched by the burden of destiny. His eyes drifted to the garden, the very one where he used to play for hours on end. The scent of the blooming flowers felt achingly familiar. He could vividly recall chasing his pets across the soft grass, their playful barks and meows filling the air. In the distance, he remembered the sparrow that always visited the garden, perching on the edge of the fountain.

It was Liya, his beloved childhood friend and teacher, who had taught him about the sparrow's significance. She had always spoken in riddles, saying, "The sparrow represents freedom, Ronaldo. To understand it, is to understand your own heart." Liya's teachings had shaped much of his early life, guiding him through difficult times, but her absence in the latter years left a void. Her words about freedom echoed in his mind now, more clearly than ever.

He knew why. She was still trapped, her fate entwined with the kingdom's dark secrets. Ronaldo clenched his fists, his heart heavy with the weight of unresolved promises. He hadn't forgotten her, nor had he forgotten the vow he made to free her from the chains that bound her. The memory of her gentle smile and the lessons they shared fueled his determination. His voice, soft yet filled with resolve, broke the silence.

"Liya," he whispered, "don't worry. I will free you. Your Ronaldo is coming." His gaze hardened as he looked up at the castle, knowing that the path ahead would not be easy. But he was ready. His past, his memories, and his love for Liya had reignited the flame within him. Nothing could stand in his way now. The time for hesitation was over. The journey to reclaim both his kingdom and Liya's freedom had begun.

Chapter # 8

Prince Ronaldo is Back

Prince Ronaldo was on a mission to reclaim his rightful place as ruler of the kingdom that had been stolen from him. Determined to regain his throne, he knew that the first step was to win the trust and support of his people. The public had to believe in him again, and he had to remind them who he was and what had happened. Ronaldo began by organizing meetings with various public groups across the kingdom. He needed to face his people directly, share his story, and gain their confidence. In every meeting, he started by introducing himself as the rightful prince, their once and future leader.

His voice carried both strength and vulnerability as he recounted the tragic tale of how he lost his kingdom. Michael, the treacherous usurper, had attacked Ronaldo's kingdom without warning. In a swift and merciless move, Michael took control, leaving the young prince powerless.

Ronaldo's survival had only been possible due to the bravery of his loyal nanny, Liya. She had protected him from harm, risking her own life to whisk him away to safety. Hidden and sheltered, the prince had grown up in exile, waiting for the day he could return to reclaim what was his. But Ronaldo had not been alone during this journey. Liya's son Darius had been with him, standing by his side through thick and thin. Together, they had grown up like brothers, forging an unbreakable bond. Now, as Ronaldo prepared to face the greatest challenge of his life, Darius was with him in every meeting, a silent but powerful reminder of the loyalty and sacrifice that had saved the prince's life.

For a month, Ronaldo tirelessly traveled from village to village, speaking to the people day after day. He shared his story with passion, his words touching the hearts of those who had once known him as a boy. Slowly, the people began to see him not just as the exiled prince, but as their future king. His determination, honesty, and courage won their respect, and they began to rally behind him.

The mission to take back his kingdom was only beginning, but Ronaldo had taken a crucial first step: he had rekindled the hope of his people, and with their support, he was ready to reclaim his throne. The public had grown weary of Michael's erratic behavior and the injustice that plagued the kingdom under his influence. Tension and discontent had spread, leaving the people longing for the peace and stability they once enjoyed. When Prince returned, it was as if a ray of hope had pierced through the darkness. His arrival sparked a collective sense of relief, and the people were quick to rally behind him.

They knew they had to support him in his mission, believing that only through unity could the kingdom be restored to its former glory. The memories of King Eric's reign lingered in the minds of the people. Under his leadership, there had been a sense of order, fairness, and harmony, a time when the kingdom thrived, and its citizens lived without fear. Everyone yearned to return to those peaceful days.

They saw in the Prince the same qualities that once defined King Eric, and they believed he was the one who could bring back the balance that had been lost. With renewed hope, the people stood ready to assist the Prince, determined to reclaim their beloved kingdom from the chaos and injustice that had overtaken it. Ronaldo entered the grand gates of the kingdom, with the public following closely behind him. His arrival caused a stir as the people whispered among themselves, amazed by his boldness.

Ronaldo, however, remained calm and determined, his eyes set on a single goal meeting the ruler of this land, Michael. He sent a message through the royal guards, wants to meet with him. When the guards relayed the message to Michael, he was taken aback. At first, he didn't believe what he was hearing. "How could Ronaldo, of all people, dare to set foot in my kingdom?"

Michael thought to himself, his face twisting in disbelief. Fury quickly replaced his surprise. Michael slammed his fist onto the arm of his throne, standing up with a look of pure disdain. "How dare he come here!" he shouted, his voice echoing through the grand halls. "He thinks he can waltz into my territory like this? I will never forgive him. I will never let him walk away unpunished!" His mind raced with anger as he remembered past conflicts with Ronaldo. For Michael, this was not just an unannounced visit; it was an affront to his authority, a challenge to his power.

Summoning his advisors and guards, he prepared for confrontation, vowing that Ronaldo's boldness would be met with fierce retribution. Michael told him to call him immediately. When he saw Ronaldo, he remarked, "I think you don't value your life, which is why you came here on your own."

His words were sharp, implying danger or poor judgment, making it clear he was concerned for Ronaldo's safety. "You sit there, thinking you're untouchable, like you've truly earned the throne you snatched from others. But every person has their limits, and not everyone is meant to rule. "You may hold the title of king now, but you've never deserved it. You took what wasn't yours, and for that, your days in the kingdom are numbered. You've caused pain, left deep wounds in your wake, thinking there would never be any consequences. But mark my words: you will know that pain soon enough. The suffering you inflicted on others will come back to you, and when it does, you won't be able to bear it".

"The weight of your actions will crush you, and I will be there to make sure of it. I'm not here for revenge out of spite or hatred. I'm here because there's an unfinished story, one you interrupted when you took what wasn't yours. You think you've won, but this story isn't over". "Far from it. You might believe that time is on your side, that your power will last forever, but power is fleeting. What's been stolen will be returned, and justice will come for you. Every wrong will be righted, and every wound you caused will be healed except for yours. You will pay for your actions in full".

"So, enjoy your reign while you can. Sit on that throne, laugh, and pretend like nothing can touch you. But know, the Prince of kingdom is back, I'm coming for what is rightfully mine, and when I do, you will wish you had never stolen the crown in the first place".

JUST WAIT......

Chapter # 9

Ronaldo VS Michael

In a grand courtyard surrounded by high walls, King Michael stood tall on his throne, overlooking the ground where a man, shackled and bruised, was brought before the roaring crowd. The guards, following the king's orders without question, dragged the prisoner to the center of the arena. Onlookers, packed tightly behind the barriers, craned their necks to catch a glimpse of the scene unfolding. The man, battered but unwavering, was no ordinary criminal.

He was Ronaldo, a figure known only to a select few for his extraordinary abilities.

Michael's eyes gleamed with malice as he addressed the crowd. "Release my dogs," he ordered coldly. "Let them tear him apart. I want a live show!" The crowd erupted into cheers, eager for the bloodsport, but Ronaldo stood calm, his eyes locked onto the king's. The gates of the arena creaked open, and a pack of snarling, ravenous dogs stormed onto the ground.

They circled Ronaldo, barking ferociously, baring their sharp teeth. Their feral hunger was unmistakable as they drew closer, saliva dripping from their jaws. But Ronaldo remained still, his gaze steady and unafraid. As the dogs lunged, something remarkable happened. Ronaldo locked eyes with the lead dog, a massive beast with dark fur and menacing eyes. In that moment, the air shifted. Ronaldo's power, subtle overwhelming, radiated outwards. Within moments, the dogs, who had been seconds away from tearing him apart, stopped in their tracks. Their growls faded, replaced by whines of confusion. One by one, they lowered their heads, as if submitting to Ronaldo's unspoken command. Then, to everyone's astonishment, the dogs sat quietly at his feet, calm and obedient.

The crowd fell silent, disbelief washing over them like a wave. What had just happened?

Murmurs spread through the spectators, and then, slowly, the silence broke into wild cheers and shouts of amazement. Ronaldo smirked, his eyes still on King Michael. "Your dogs are no match for me," he said, his voice laced with confidence. "Perhaps you should try yourself."

Furious, Michael's face turned red. Enraged by the humiliation and the defiance in Ronaldo's voice, he stormed down from his throne and entered the arena himself. His pride and authority were on the line, and he was ready to fight. Prince Ronaldo and Michael stood face to face, their intense rivalry evident in their steely glares. The crowd had gathered, murmuring in anticipation, their voices a constant hum of support for their beloved prince. Michael, tall, powerful, and brimming with physical strength, had initiated the confrontation by striking Ronaldo, sending a shockwave through the onlookers.

His blow was fierce, a clear display of his dominance. But Ronaldo, calm and composed, held back from retaliating immediately. His resolve to prevent himself from hitting back was not out of fear but of patience. Ronaldo wasn't as physically imposing as Michael, but he had something far greater mental strength. His years of suffering had shaped him, giving him an unshakable inner fortitude. Michael had caused Ronaldo immense pain over the years, driving a wedge between him and his loved ones, distancing him from his family, and leaving his heart burned with the memory of Liya's anguish.

Ronaldo's parents had been hurt, and their wounds, both physical and emotional, haunted him. Yet, their unwavering love, prayers, and support had always been his source of strength. In this moment, as he prepared to face his opponent, those memories fueled him, reminding him why he needed to win.

The crowd, fervent in their support for their prince, chanted Ronaldo's name, their voices growing louder with each passing second. It was clear that the people were on his side. Their encouragement, combined with the love of his parents and his memories of Liya, strengthened his resolve. This fight was not just a physical battle; it was deeply personal.

Michael charged forward, his powerful physique making each of his strikes deadly and precise. He fought with brute force, attempting to overpower Ronaldo, hoping to crush him as he had done to others before. But Ronaldo, agile and focused, dodged most of the blows, his mind sharp, his reflexes quicker than Michael anticipated.

While Michael's physical strength was formidable, Ronaldo's mental strength was impenetrable. As the fight dragged on, it became a grueling test of endurance. Michael's hits were forceful, but Ronaldo's defense was unbreakable. He fought not only with his body but with his heart and mind. Every time he felt himself weakening, he thought of his parents' love, their prayers for his.victory, and the suffering he had endured because of Michael's cruelty.

The pain from his past fueled his strength, giving him a second wind when he needed it most. After what felt like an eternity, Ronaldo saw his opportunity. With the crowd roaring in approval, he launched a decisive blow, throwing Michael off balance. In one swift motion, he grabbed Michael and hurled him onto the floor. The thud echoed through the arena as Michael crashed down, fainting from the impact.

The fight was over. Prince Ronaldo stood victorious, his chest heaving as the weight of the battle lifted from his shoulders. The public erupted in cheers, their voices full of pride and joy for their prince. Ronaldo, though bruised and tired, smiled faintly. He had won, not just against Michael, but against the darkness of his past. Prince Ronaldo's reign was now secure. His loyal soldiers had arrested Michael, and his guards had been subdued and taken into custody. Order was swiftly restored across the kingdom, and Ronaldo assumed full control of his realm.

Yet, one thought consumed Ronaldo's mind Liya. He turned to his guards with urgency in his voice. "Find her. Now!" he commanded. Hours later, she was found, bound and frail, in the dark confines of a prison cell. Her once youthful vibrancy had faded, and age and suffering weighed heavily on her. When they brought her out, Ronaldo could hardly recognize the woman who had once been a guiding light in his life. He approached her slowly, his heart aching at the sight of her fragile frame. Overcome with emotion, he rushed forward and embraced her tightly. "Liya, it's me,"he whispered, his voice cracking. "I am your Ronaldo."

For a long moment, neither could speak, their tears expressing the depth of their pain and relief. After all these years, they were finally together again. "I am alive today because of you," Ronaldo said through his sobs. "You protected me with your honesty and loyalty, even when it cost you your freedom".

Liya gazed at him, her weary eyes brimming with love and sorrow. "You deserved better, not this," Ronaldo continued, his voice filled with emotion. "You were imprisoned for years because of your integrity, and for that, you deserve love, not suffering." They held each other close, their tears mingling with years of unspoken words and unshed pain. In that moment, they both knew that they had found something far greater than a kingdom they had found each other again.

Chapter # 10

Happly Ending

Prince Ronaldo stood on the balcony of his castle, overlooking the kingdom he had fought so hard to reclaim. The sun bathed the land in a golden hue, and the air was filled with the sound of joy and peace. After months of turmoil, the kingdom had finally found stability. The people were happy, and Ronaldo's heart swelled with pride knowing he had restored the kingdom to its former glory, just as his father, King Eric, had once ruled. He had also invited his beloved adopted parents to live in the castle with him, where they would now stay forever. Their presence brought him comfort, knowing they had always been by his side, even in the darkest moments.

The kingdom flourished under Ronaldo's reign. His father's legacy guided his every decision, and the people loved him for it. The harmony of the kingdom reflected the peaceful environment that now thrived, the echoes of war and strife a distant memory. Yet, despite the triumph, something weighed on his mind, a memory he could not shake Anna, who had betrayed him.

Anna had held Ronaldo captive for months, using him as a pawn for her personal ambitions. She was a well known interviewer, ruthless and calculating, someone who would stop at nothing to climb the ladder of success. To her, Ronaldo had been just another means to an end. She never saw him as a person with emotions or dreams just another opportunity to advance her career.

But something had changed in Anna during the time Ronaldo was imprisoned. She had been forced to confront the truth about herself, about the way she had used people without considering the consequences of her actions. The realization had come with a heavy price she had lost everything, including her integrity.

She was filled with regret, ashamed of how she had hurt so many, especially Ronaldo, the man she now realized meant more to her than anyone else. Determined to make amends, Anna traveled to the kingdom. Her heart pounded as she stood before the castle gates, unsure if Ronaldo would even agree to see her. But she had to try, no matter the cost.

When she was finally granted an audience with the king, Anna could barely look Ronaldo in the eyes. He stood tall and regal, his face calm, yet unreadable. She knelt before him, tears welling.in her eyes. "I'm so sorry, Your Majesty," she whispered. "I was wrong. I used you for my own selfish reasons. I never. understood your feelings, never cared about how I hurt you. I was so focused on my job that I forgot about the people behind the interviews. But you...you showed me the truth, and for that, I am truly ashamed."

Ronaldo watched her in silence, his expression softening as she continued. "I have changed. I see now how wrong I was, not just with you, but with so many others. I know I don't deserve your forgiveness, but I have to ask. I...I have feelings for you now. Please, give me one more chance."

The room fell silent, and Anna's heart raced as she awaited his response. Ronaldo sighed deeply, his gaze searching hers. After what felt like an eternity, he spoke, his voice steady yet kind. Ronaldo looked into her eyes and saw the sincerity they held. He felt deep within that she wasn't lying, that her words were genuine. Trusting his intuition, he decided to forgive her, letting go of his doubts and embracing the truth he believed she was telling.

"Anna, I appreciate your apology. I can see that you've changed, and I'm glad you have realized the harm you caused. Forgiveness...that is not something that can be granted easily. But I believe in second chances." But remember, trust is fragile. It must be earned, not demanded." Tears of relief and gratitude filled Anna' s eyes. "Thank you," she whispered. In the heart of the Royal Kingdom, a vibrant new chapter began.

After a prolonged period of gloom and uncertainty, the morning sun finally pierced through the clouds, bathing the kingdom in a bright, hopeful light. The atmosphere was filled with optimism as the people embraced the change, their spirits lifted by the promise of new beginnings.

Ronaldo, a key figure in this evolving tale, lived a fulfilling life with his beloved Liya and their young son. His parents, who had been pillars of strength throughout the kingdom's trials, were also by his side, adding warmth and wisdom to their daily lives. The family was the epitome of unity and joy, their home a sanctuary of peace amidst the surrounding changes.

Amidst the backdrop of this renewed vitality, a significant event was on the horizon: the marriage of Ronaldo and Anna. The union was not just a personal milestone for them but a symbol of the kingdom's return to prosperity and harmony. Their wedding was a grand celebration, with the entire kingdom rejoicing in their happiness. The ceremony was a blend of regal splendor and heartfelt emotion, reflecting the deep bond between the two and their commitment to each other.

As Ronaldo and Anna prepared to step into their new roles, the kingdom was transitioning into a new era of peace and stability. The people, once weary from the struggles and upheavals, now looked forward to a future brimming with hope and promise. The completion of the royal lineage with the marriage of Ronaldo and Anna signified the kingdom's return to its former glory.

In this new chapter, the kingdom was not just a place of residence but a thriving realm of joy and contentment. The king and queen, with their shared vision and dedication, promised a reign marked by prosperity and harmony. Their leadership was set to guide the kingdom through an age of peace, where every challenge was met with resilience and every joy was celebrated with exuberance.

The story of the Royal Kingdom, with all its ups and downs, struggles, and triumphs, had come to a gratifying conclusion. It was a tale of perseverance and renewal, where the trials of the past gave way to a future filled with promise. The kingdom, now complete with its king and queen, stood as a testament to the enduring spirit of its people and the hopeful horizons that lay ahead. The story concluded with joy and fulfillment, characters embraced their dreams, and everything resolved. perfectly, leaving hearts content.

ABOUT AUTHOR

As a clinical psychologist, I have devoted my career to understanding and addressing the complexities of the human mind. My experience spans across various areas, including addiction, adult psychology, and child psychology. Over the years, I have worked with individuals from diverse backgrounds, each carrying their own set of challenges and trauma. One thing that has become increasingly clear to me is that psychological illnesses are rarely caused by a single event or factor. Instead, they are often the result of multiple underlying causes that intertwine to create emotional and mental distress. Trauma, for instance, can stem from a variety of sources, such as past experiences, family dynamics, environmental influences, and even unresolved emotional conflicts. These layers of pain often manifest in ways that may not be immediately obvious, and understanding the root cause is essential in helping individuals heal. In my practice, I have learned that overcoming these deeply ingrained issues requires more than just clinical interventions. While therapy and medication can play significant roles, I believe that storytelling is a powerful tool that can inspire change and healing. Stories have the ability to connect us, to make us feel understood, and to give us hope. By sharing the stories of others who have faced and overcome similar struggles, I hope to provide my patients with a sense of empowerment. My goal is to enable people to see that, no matter how difficult their situation may seem, there is always a way forward. Recovery is not an easy journey, but it is a possible one. In my approach, I focus on helping individuals uncover the factors that contribute to their psychological distress. Whether it's unresolved childhood trauma, addiction, or anxiety stemming from life's pressures, I work with my patients to explore these issues in depth. By doing so, we can identify the root cause of their struggles and begin the healing process. I emphasize the importance of self-awareness, self-compassion, and the development of healthy coping mechanisms. These elements are crucial for long-term mental health and well-being. In addition to my professional work, I also have a passion for personal growth and exploration. My hobbies include writing, traveling, gardening, cooking and learning new skills. These activities allow me to stay grounded and maintain balance in my life. Traveling, in particular, gives me a broader perspective on different cultures and how mental health is perceived and treated globally. Reading helps me continuously learn, while cooking provides a creative outlet where I can unwind and express myself. Through my practice and storytelling, I aim to encourage people to confront their challenges, understand the many factors that contribute to their mental health, and ultimately live healthier, more fulfilling lives. It is my hope that by sharing these stories, others will feel empowered to begin their own journey toward healing and self-discovery.

SUNDAS SHAKEEL

Don't miss out!

Visit the website below and you can sign up to receive emails whenever Sundas Shakeel publishes a new book. There's no charge and no obligation.

https://books2read.com/r/B-A-GLYOC-RSRFF

BOOKS 2 READ

Connecting independent readers to independent writers.

www.ingramcontent.com/pod-product-compliance
Lightning Source LLC
Chambersburg PA
CBHW071245130726
47998CB00003B/1066